I cannot wait for you to see
how **great** the world can be . . .

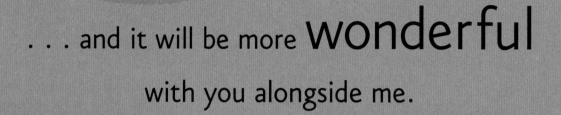

. . . and it will be more wonderful

with you alongside me.

I cannot wait to **teach** you
how to do the things I do.

I'll share and show all that I know
and **learn** new things from you.

Side by side,

we'll walk the world.

We'll make a super team!

And troubles shared are **never**

quite as bad as they first seem.

And one day not so far from now,

you'll walk ahead of me.

I'll watch your steps with happiness.
I know how **proud** I'll be.

And even when you're quite grown-up
and life's in front of you . . .

. . . what I'll **wish** for most . . .

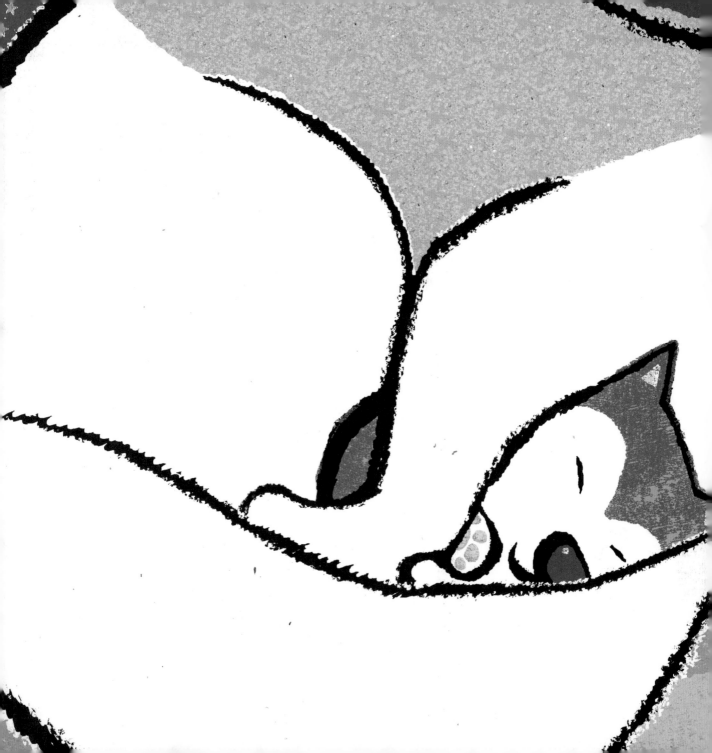